# MR PATTACAKE

### Stephanie Baudet

# Sweet Cherry
## Publishing

Published by Sweet Cherry Publishing Limited
Unit 36, Vulcan House
Vulcan Road
Leicester, LE5 3EF
United Kingdom

First published in the UK in 2017
ISBN: 978-1-78226-257-2
©Stephanie Baudet 2015
Illustrations ©Creative Books
Illustrated by Joyson Loitongbam

Mr Pattacake and the Great Cake Bake Competition

Wai Man Book Binding (China) Ltd. Kowloon, H.K.

Pattacake, Pattacake, baker's man,
Bake me a cake as fast as you can;
Pat it and prick it and mark it with P,
Put it in the oven for you and for me.

Pattacake, Pattacake, baker's man,
Bake me a cake as fast as you can;
Roll it up, roll it up;
And throw it in a pan!

Pattacake, Pattacake, baker's man.

# MR PATTACAKE
## and the
# GREAT CAKE BAKE
# COMPETITION

'I've done it!' shouted Mr Pattacake one morning, waving a letter in the air. He began to do the silly dance he always did when he was excited. In fact, he danced from the hall all the way through to the kitchen where his lazy ginger cat, Treacle, was *trying* to have a quiet after-breakfast nap.

'I'm one of the **finalists!**' Mr Pattacake
exclaimed as his big chef's hat wobbled furiously.

Treacle stirred, listening without opening his eyes. His ears twitched. It didn't sound like the usual cooking job Mr Pattacake was asked to do, and Treacle had no idea at all what a finalist was.

Mr Pattacake, who had been around cats all his life, and Treacle for several years, always knew what he was thinking.

'I'm the finalist in the television chef competition,' he explained, out of breath from all that dancing. 'Don't you remember, Treacle? The prize is to have your own television cooking series. Something I've always dreamed about!'

Treacle opened one eye to look at Mr Pattacake.

'Chefs from all over the country had to send in their CVs,' Mr Pattacake went on. 'Oh come on, Treacle, show a little excitement for me!'

Treacle sensed something was expected of him. He sat up, looked Mr Pattacake in the eye and tried to look as though he was interested.

Mr Pattacake sat down on a chair. 'So I sent them my CV. I told them all about the jobs I've… *we've* done.' He quickly added, 'Like the time we went to Switzerland for the children's skiing party, the time we cooked for the circus – and the pirate ship as well. Do you remember that, Treacle?'

Treacle shuddered. How could he forget? He'd had to walk the plank and he'd got *very* wet. And that awful parrot had kept pecking at him.

'I mentioned it all in my CV, and now I have been chosen as one of the five finalists. We have to go to the annual *Great Cake Bake Competition* and bake a simple sponge cake.'

Mr Pattacake reached out for a piece of paper and a pen. He always made a list whenever he had a cooking job, and this was no exception. Making lists made sure that nothing was forgotten.

After a while, Mr Pattacake looked up from his list. 'My granny was good at sponge cakes,' he said. 'In fact, she won many competitions with them. Light as air, people would say. They could almost float away on their own. Come to think of it, she said she had a secret ingredient. She never did tell me what it was. I wonder…'

He got up from the table and climbed up into the loft. Somewhere in here was his granny's old wooden chest.

After moving all the Christmas decorations to the side, as well as two old suitcases, Mr Pattacake found the chest. He dragged it out under the light. Then he opened the lid, coughing as the dust flew everywhere.

Inside he found lots of old recipe books, battered and well used, as well as several cooking certificates and awards.

There was a photo too, of Granny being given a prize for one of her sponge cakes. There she stood, smiling broadly and standing in front of a table on which her cake was displayed, complete with first prize rosette.

Under the photo he found an envelope with his name on it.

*For Percy, with love from Granny.*

Just what he was looking for!

For Percy, with love from Granny

Inside was a single sheet of faded writing.

Solve these riddles and you will discover four words, all of which contain the secret ingredient for making the lightest sponge cakes in the world.

1.   I have legs and feet
     But cannot run
     And arms,
     and back and seat

2.   I cannot move though I'm alive
     I grow and grow
     Long and thin
     Thousands of us side by side

3.  *We always go in twos*
    *Like twins*
    *Or pants*
    *Or shoes*

4.  *Lots of fun*
    *With rides and*
    *Candyfloss*
    *And prizes won*

Mr Pattacake peered at the riddles again, confused. He then folded the sheet and put it in the pocket of his big white apron. He put the trunk back where he'd found it, and went back downstairs. These riddles were going to take some time to solve.

When he was back in the kitchen again, Mr Pattacake waved the sheet of paper at Treacle. 'You'll *have* to help me with these, Treacle.'

But Treacle just curled into a tighter ball and closed his eyes. Whoever heard of a cat that could solve riddles?

Time went by, and the day of the competition drew nearer. Still Mr Pattacake had not solved the riddles so he decided to ask some of the children whose birthdays he had cooked for.

He must solve the riddles and discover Granny's secret ingredient otherwise he would have no chance of winning the prize. He now knew who the other contestants were. Four very famous chefs. Oliver James, Laurie Nigel, Smithy Dells and Martina Jamieson.

What chance could Mr Pattacake have against *them*?

Well, he would try, anyway. You could never succeed if you didn't try.

Danny and Alice and Sally and Jack came round with their mums and they all sat down to try to work out the riddles. Mr Pattacake had to admit that he might be good at cooking but he was not good at puzzles.

They looked at the first one.

*I have legs and feet*

*But cannot run*

*And arms,*

*and back and seat*

'It's a baby,' said Jack. 'They have legs and feet but cannot run, and they have arms.'

'They have a back, too,' said Danny. 'But not a seat.'

'Well, they have a bottom,' said Jack, laughing.

'I know what it is.' They all looked at Sally. 'It's a chair.'

Mr Pattacake nodded enthusiastically and wrote it down on a piece of paper. 'Now for the second one.'

*I cannot move though I'm alive*

*I grow and grow*

*Long and thin*

*Thousands of us side by side*

'Snakes!' said Alice.

'You don't get *thousands* of them,' said Danny with a shudder.

'Maybe grass,' said Jack's mum.

'Could be,' said Mr Pattacake. 'But you wouldn't put grass into a sponge cake.'

'Or a chair,' said Alice.

Mr Pattacake shook his head and sighed. This was turning out to be impossible.

'Let's try number three instead,' he said.

*We always go in twos*

*Like twins*

*Or pants*

*Or shoes*

'Pair!' said Alice's mum, cheerfully.

Mr Pattacake wrote it down. 'Now the last one,' he said.

> *Lots of fun*
> *With rides and*
> *Candyfloss*
> *And prizes won*

'Fair!' exclaimed Jack. 'That must mean the second one must be hair. They all rhyme.'

Mr Pattacake beamed and looked at his list. 'Chair, hair, pair and fair. My Granny said that they all had the magic ingredient in them. What could it be?'

'Air!' they all chorused.

'Of course! They must have *plenty* of air in them to make them rise. That's what will make the perfect sponge cake!'

Mr Pattacake cheered. He stood up and did his silly dance all around the room, his big chef's hat wobbling dangerously as he wiggled his way past an unimpressed Treacle.

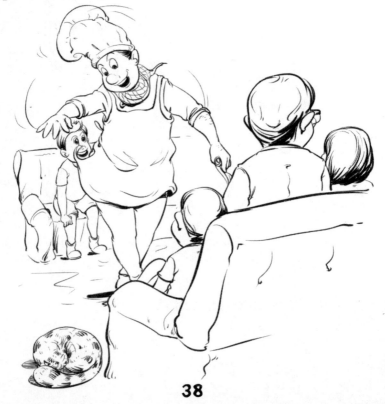

Everyone laughed and tucked in to the chocolate mice that Mr Pattacake had made that morning. Treacle, however, barely lifted a paw. He had had his fill of broken bits that had dropped on the floor (even though everyone knows that chocolate is bad for cats).

When the day of the competition came, Mr Pattacake and Treacle got up early. A clean white apron and newly starched big chef's hat were laid out carefully on top of the boxes that were filled with everything he would need.

When they had eaten breakfast, Mr Pattacake flung open the doors of his little yellow van, ready to load it up.

He had left the van doors open while fetching his big box, so he didn't notice when a certain mischievous little tortoiseshell cat leapt softly into the van and hid in an unseen corner. She curled up into a tight ball, resting her head on her front paws and smiling a smug cat's smile. She *definitely* wasn't going to miss out on *this* event.

It was quite a long way to the town where the competition was being held, but Mr Pattacake and Treacle arrived in plenty of time. A big marquee had been set up, and inside were five identical brand new ovens, all connected to electric extension cables from a nearby building. The competition had to be completely fair after all.

Mr Pattacake unloaded his boxes onto a table, taking care not to crease his apron and big chef's hat.

He and Treacle then went to a nearby chicken farm to buy some fresh eggs. The organisers had insisted that they were ones that had just been laid that morning, and Mr Pattacake knew that fresh, unchilled eggs were very important to the success of a good sponge cake.

The chickens seemed to be a little afraid of Treacle, and clucked and squawked as he walked past their enormous pen.

'Now,' said Mr Pattacake, arriving back at the marquee, 'Time to prepare.' He put on the big, clean, white apron and big chef's hat, which wobbled as his excitement mounted.

The other four chefs had arrived too, and were greeting each other with a professional nod. The two judges took their seats behind a table and the crowd jostled for a good position. Many people had brought chairs to sit on too.

Treacle retreated to a corner of the marquee and lay down as if to sleep, though his eyes weren't *completely* shut of course – he needed to keep an eye on Mr Pattacake, just in case any cake bits dropped on the floor. He would be a helpful cat and help to clean up.

The crowd went quiet. The chefs stood by their tables, ready to go, and the judges looked at their watches. Then one of them said:

'Ladies and gentlemen, please settle down. Contestants, you have forty-five minutes. May the best chef win – ready, steady, BAKE!'

Mr Pattacake started by laying out his bowl, his wooden spoon and metal spoon, and his hand whisk. They were not allowed to use any electric equipment, except for the ovens, of course.

He put out his digital scales and his oven thermometer, and greased his baking tin. He then turned on the oven, making sure that the shelf was in the middle.

He began to weigh the ingredients. His granny had always said that a good chef *weighed* the ingredients, not *measured* them. It was more accurate. He separated the eggs, yolks and whites going into different bowls.

First, in went the flour. He'd bought the very finest cake flour for a lighter cake. When he'd weighed it he had sifted it *three* times to add even more air. Into the flour went the caster sugar and butter. The butter was soft as he had placed it in the sun on the drive here – soft, but not runny.

He could hear his granny's words in his head. Of course, Mr Pattacake had made many sponge cakes before, but never had they been so important, so this time he had to take special care – he had a competition to win!

He glanced across at the other chefs. They were already beating their mixtures. He would have to hurry, yet he knew that a cake couldn't be rushed. A calm, happy chef produces a lighter cake, Granny used to say.

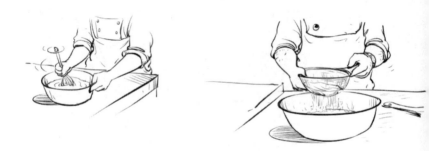

Mr Pattacake reached for his mixing bowl and tipped in the sugar and egg yolks. He beat them together with the whisk until they were a creamy and lemony colour.

Then he whisked the egg whites until they formed peaks and slowly folded the egg yolk mixture into it. He began to worry as he added in the sifted flour – did he have enough time?

It was now time for the secret ingredient – air. He folded it in, trapping it in the mixture. Slowly and carefully. He knew he must not rush, yet it was difficult when time was going so quickly.

By the time he had carefully mixed in the rest of the ingredients the other chefs had already put their cakes in the oven.

Mr Pattacake looked at his watch, worriedly. Only twenty minutes to go – and the cake would take twenty-five minutes to bake.

**Oh dribble !** He was late!

He slowly poured the mixture into the baking tin and then tested the temperature in the oven. A little hot. He turned it down a notch, leaving the door open while he fetched the cake tin. It was now a perfect temperature – so in it went finally.

Mr Pattacake straightened up and sighed heavily. Was it too late? Was there enough time left for his cake to bake? If there wasn't, he would have wasted his time and lost the competition.

His chance of doing a television series would have gone.

The other chefs were watching him and looking confident. After all, a sponge cake was an easy thing to bake. They could all have made something much more difficult and worthy of their experience.

Treacle was also watching Mr Pattacake. He saw that he was anxious and that his cake had gone in last, after all the other chefs.

Now, Mr Pattacake would never cheat. It was a thought that wouldn't even enter his head. He tried to be absolutely fair at all times. But Treacle did not have such high morals. He would do anything to get his own way, even if it meant cheating.

He was a cat, after all, and they did tend to be a little selfish and had absolutely no manners.

If Mr Pattacake needed a few extra minutes for his cake to bake, then he, Treacle, would provide them. He got up, stretched, and then scuttled away without anyone noticing. That is, except for a pair of yellow eyes that didn't miss anything, and whose owner had been watching every move.

Naughty Tortie got up and followed Treacle to see what he was up to.

Treacle ran to the chicken farm. The chickens clucked loudly and strutted about restlessly when they saw him. Treacle looked at the gate to the chicken run. Now, some clever cats have been known to learn how to open doors, and Treacle was one of those.

He jumped onto the top of the gate. Then he lifted the little hook with his teeth, and expertly wiggled it out of the loop. Jumping down onto the ground again, he gave the gate a push with his paw and it swung open.

Chickens, on the other hand, are not as clever as cats, so it took them a moment to notice that the gate was open, and another moment to muster up the courage to go through it.

Meanwhile, Treacle had gone and taken a huge mouthful of grain from the chicken's trough. Then, running out of the gate, he began to sprinkle the grain in a little trail straight to the marquee where the competition was taking place, and especially to the oven in which Mr Pattacake's cake was baking.

Mr Pattacake was looking at his watch again, and so were the judges. Any minute now they would end the competition. The other chefs were already putting on their oven gloves and moving towards the ovens to take out their cakes.

Mr Pattacake watched as the first cake came out. It had risen beautifully and was golden in colour. Baked to perfection. The other three chefs took out their cakes and placed them on plates on the judging table. They looked perfect too. It would be a difficult job to judge the winner.

I've lost, thought Mr Pattacake, a sinking feeling in his stomach. It was no use taking his cake out now because he knew it wouldn't be baked yet. He had spent too much time in the preparation. He should have worked his timing out better, and maybe even had a few rehearsals at home. Oh well, I guess this is the end of it, he thought with a heavy heart.

Just then, he heard a big noise coming from across the field.

**CLUCK CLUCK**

Mr Pattacake and everyone else looked up to see a tide of chickens swarming towards the marquee, squawking and cackling as they fought for the grain. The four chefs whose cakes were on the table just had time to cover them with upturned tins before the mass of chickens poured into the marquee, pecking at the ground as they went. Squabbling and clucking, they fluttered and hopped on top of each other, onto the worktops, and even onto the judges' table, where one of them did a poop. What a mess!

The judges leapt to their feet, but not before one hen had flown up and landed on one of their heads, scrabbling to try and get a hold on the bald shiny surface. The judge waved his arms wildly, running in circles to try and shake it off. 'Get off!' He tried to run but the hen clung on bravely.

The air was filled with chaos and feathers flew. Meanwhile, Mr Pattacake's cake quietly rose in the oven. He didn't know what to make of it at all, but it was certainly lucky for him. He couldn't possibly get near the oven to take out his cake because the chickens were knee-deep in front of it.

When Treacle thought the time was right, he began to herd the chickens out of the marquee and back towards the farm. Naughty Tortie ran to help, and before long all except a few stragglers were back home, where the surprised farmer finally got them back in their run and firmly closed the gate.

People in the crowd cheered Treacle and Naughty Tortie when they returned.

What good cats they had been – chasing the chickens away. No one, not even Mr Pattacake, knew that it had been Treacle who had let them out in the first place!

The judges brushed themselves down and shook their heads as if they couldn't quite believe what had just happened. Mr Pattacake picked up his oven gloves, opened the oven door, and lifted out his cake.

When the small crowd of people saw the cake, they gasped.

The other chefs uncovered their cakes, which had fortunately not been damaged by the chicken invasion, and Mr Pattacake placed his next to theirs.

It had risen far more. In fact, it had risen twice as much as the others. Everyone gazed at it in wonder. But that, alone, would not make him the winner. The cakes also had to *taste* good.

Carefully, the judges cut a small slice from each cake and popped them into their mouths, one at a time. They chewed slowly and closed their eyes while the chefs and the audience watched in silence, holding their breath.

Two cats sat side by side watching too.

When the judges had lifted up the cakes and looked at them from all angles, and when they had poked and prodded them and then tasted them, they went back to their table and had a little talk.

At last, one of them said, 'We have decided that the outstanding winner of this competition is…'

'Mr Percy Pattacake!'

A big cheer went up and Mr Pattacake felt dizzy with surprise and pride. He had won! He was to have his own television show.

When the applause had died down the other judge said, 'Congratulations, Mr Pattacake, your cake was delicious, and as light as AIR.'

'Yes,' agreed the other judge. 'It was the best sponge cake I have ever tasted. Absolutely as light as…' He looked around for the right word.

'As light as a FEATHER!'

Mr Pattacake did his silly dance right there in front of the judges, the other chefs and all the people, and his big chef's hat wobbled so much that it fell right off his head.

The rival chefs all shook hands with him and then the cakes were cut and pieces handed out for everybody to eat.

Under the table Treacle and Naughty Tortie nibbled at the crumbs that fell, sometimes they accidentally ate some of the grain that Treacle had scattered for the chickens too.

By the time they had polished off all of the crumbs, there was no trace of the grain at all. Treacle and Naughty Tortie smiled a secret smile at each other.

Once everyone had celebrated, and they were all back at home, Mr Pattacake sat down at the kitchen table and began to make a list of all the dishes that he was planning to cook on his television show.

Now and again, he paused and thought back over the strange day, and the chickens escaping just at the right moment to delay the judges ending the competition.

He glanced over to Treacle, curled up in his bed. He had been the hero, he and Naughty Tortie, because they had rounded up the chickens and herded them back to the farm.

But he couldn't have had anything to do with letting them out, could he?

No! He was only a cat.

Treacle smiled his cat's smile.